BEAR CLAUS

A Bear Jacobs
Holiday Novella

Linda B. Myers

About This Novella

Bear Claus is a work of fiction. Names, characters, places and happenings are from the author's imagination. Any resemblance to actual persons – living or dead – events, or locales is entirely coincidental.

Published 2015 by Mycomm One. Revised 2017

ISBN: 978-0-9986747-4-2

Cover design by IntroStudio.me

For updates, news, blog and chatter:

www.LindaBMyers.com

www.amazon.com/author/lindabmyers

Facebook.com/lindabmyers.author

Twitter.com/LindaBMyers

Dedication

For my sister, Donna Whichello.

Bear doesn't have a clue without her help.

CHAPTER ONE

Case Notes
December 8, 11 a.m.

I have nothing to say.
It's the fault of that retired pile of ursine melancholy, PI Bear Ja-
cobs. Even on his best days, observers could be forgiven for thinking
of him as a cane-wielding, king-sized, potty-mouthed grouch. But
now? Right here, up against the ho-ho-holidays? The big man is a
beacon of gloom and doom, a grump who wouldn't just steal Christ-
mas, he'd ram it into the trash and set it on fire.
Bear says to leave him alone with his seasonal depression. He wants
to hibernate through the 'whole damn tinsel-covered mess.' The oth-
er residents and staff cut a wide swath around him, hoping he'll be
okay again when the tree is taken back out of the Latin's Ranch liv-
ing room, and twinkly bulbs no longer circle the dining room crown
moulding.
But I know he'd really rather join the fun. So it's up to me to poke
the bear, so to speak. All he needs is a mystery to solve. That would
make him festive as a cup of Christmas punch. If I'm going to be
his eWatson and keep his case notes, I better find him something to
scratch his head about. Otherwise, I might slip into a pile of useless-
ness myself.
I believe a mystery may be coming through the door very soon now.
My physical therapist Ernie let it slip that his girlfriend Clarice, who

is also our bookkeeper, is worried about unexplained goings on involving Eunice Taylor. Worry about my roommate is a worry for me, too. And unexplained goings on? Bingo! A mystery for Bear.

I've arranged for tea to be served in the living room after lunch. Gives us residents a chance to be alone with our guest. And for the mystery to unfold. That means I should have a lot to say any time now.

- Lily Gilbert, Jolly Assistant to PI Bear Jacobs

Clarice Hagadorn counted her blessings. Her independent bookkeeping business was burgeoning; her son managed not to flunk out his first year of college, and it appeared he might actually be growing up; she loved birding expeditions; nobody ruled her roost except the two Siamese cats, Kit Kat and Hershey, who clawed, bit, yowled and purred their way through her life; she had an ongoing relationship with a very sweet man.

From nearly every point of view, Clarice was a successful woman. But if anyone asked her, she'd say her greatest accomplishment had been the loss of seventy pounds. She could now bend over and put her palms flat on the floor. She could reach far enough to shave her legs all the way around. She could cross them, one right over the other. Her upper arms didn't flap in the breeze. The two cats no longer fit in her lap at the same time. She could hike the trails of the Cascades. She felt in shape, strong and lithe.

Clarice had not only taken it off but was keeping it off. Until now. And here it was again, a dieter's greatest dread. The downfall of all foodies. Nightmare on Loser Street.

Yes. It was the holiday season. Chestnuts roasting. Figgy puddings baking. Sugar plums dancing. Partridges in pear trees. Nogged eggs and uncontrolled wassailing. It was hearty food and drink time, and Clarice was not feeling all that grateful about it. She was on her way to Latin's Ranch to visit her client, Eunice Taylor. And since Latin's Ranch was also a client, she'd been invited to lunch. A lunch prepared by that Mexican marvel, Aurora. It would no doubt include cheese and crispy fried things and roasted pork and cream. It would be heaven on earth.

Clarice shook in the new, smaller-sized boots that fit her now trim calves.

Would it also be her nemesis from a formerly plump point of view? Would the holidays put her in the kind of tailspin that could easily lead to the fat suit again? Heaven knows, she hated to impart the news she had for Eunice. It was enough to make her stomach growl for a wee bit of comfort food.

✦ ✦ ✦

If there was one thing that could lure Bear out of his den during the holidays, it was Aurora's cooking. At Christmas time, she created a minor miracle every day of the month. It was her holiday gift to the residents and staff at Latin's Ranch Adult Care Home. The evening before she'd served their cocoa with her *buñuelos*, each little fritter sprinkled with powdered sugar. It had been almost enough to make him smile.

Monday's lunch had been *pozole*, a hearty soup of hominy, pork, chili and garlic. Today, according to the posted menu the residents checked every morning, the entree was chicken with black *mole* sauce. Aurora made hers spicy and sweet, with chocolate, cinnamon, clove and so many other surprises.

Bear was glad they had a luncheon guest. Everyone liked Clarice so chatting with her would draw their attention away from his funk. He could enjoy his *mole* in peace. He couldn't believe the reasonable portions that were keeping Clarice content. He remembered when she could out-wolf him. The woman would be an inspiration if, in fact, anything could inspire him at the moment. Maybe after lunch he'd think about the connection between food and fitness. Then again, maybe not.

Alita, their youngest aide, served them tea in the living room following lunch. The four other residents included Bear's roommate Charlie Barker, Lily, Eunice and retired capo Frankie Sapienza. Clarice joined them there. Bear thought he saw conflict in the bookkeeper's usually open and friendly face. He wondered what was up. Not that he really cared, of course.

"Lunch was lovely," Clarice said. "But Eunice, remember we need to talk for a moment before I leave."

"Okay, my dear. Talk away."

Clarice colored a pink blush that did her auburn hair no favors. "Well, I ... um ... it involves your finances, of course, and might be a bit personal if you'd like to go ..."

"Oh, heavens no, dear." Eunice made an expansive gesture with her spindly arms to include the gang. "Everyone here knows all there is to know about me, including how I look before make-up in the mornings."

Bear saw a ghost of a smile cross Lily's lips. It made him wonder if he'd actually ever seen the carefully coiffed, jewelry bedazzled Eunice before she was good and ready for her close-up. Eunice might put on airs as ditzy, but he'd learned long ago that the octogenarian had plenty of marbles under that spiky orange hair.

"Well, still ..."

"Come along, speak up girl, no mumbling," Eunice urged.

Bear watched as Clarice cleared her throat, donned a cloak of professionalism and began. "I'm aware that you do a certain amount of shopping at My Fair Pair, have for as long as I've known you."

"Yes, that's right. Lovely things they have for day or night." Eunice tucked in her chin and glanced sideways at Frankie.

This time, Bear and Charlie also concealed their smiles. All the residents knew Frankie was over the moon about Eunice. The two had been an item damn near since the day Latin's Ranch opened its doors as an adult care home.

Bear considered Eunice's purchase of lady geegaws and scanties and other unknowns to be none of his business. Charlie was more likely interested in that kind of crap since the old sumbitch was known to have an eye for the ladies. At the moment, Charlie was petting Furball, the fat cat draped across his exceptionally skinny knees, but Bear assumed he was listening with great interest.

Clarice soldiered on. "Well, recently, it seems to me your purchases have increased. They were under $50 a month. But that's been going up. In October alone, you spent over $300. And I thought, I mean, I wondered, well ..."

"You wondered how many pairs of fancy pants one old woman could need."

"Exactly!" Clarice said, following it up with an exhale that sounded like relief to Bear. "So I have to question whether someone there is fiddling with your charge account."

"Of course there is, my dear. Has for some time."

Everyone stopped what they were doing and stared at Eunice.

"Huh?" said Clarice.

"I'll second that," said Lily. "Huh?"

"Well, of course I know about it. I go over my bills quite carefully, you know. And yes it has increased here in the fourth quarter before the holidays."

Finally, Bear couldn't take it. He may have withdrawn from the group temporarily, but he'd be damned if he'd let them withdraw from him. "Eunice, if you knew about it, why didn't you tell me? Ask me to figure out what's going on? I've been known to solve a crime or two, you know. I could stop it."

"But Bear, I don't want to stop it."

"Then I, too, must ask, 'Huh?'"

"Someone steal from you, my little dove? I have his head for this," seethed the old capo.

"No, no, no! Nobody will have anybody's head. Louella Bowles has owned that store for decades. She's been my friend for decades, too. Now her daughter works there. I don't want to let Louella know someone's stealing from me. Don't want to hurt her. Don't want to accuse her daughter or any other clerk for that matter. I'd rather just pay the extra as long as it doesn't get any more out of hand."

Eunice got up from the hard backed chair she favored, flapping her wings like a sparrow in a birdbath. "And since that is my wish, Clarice I want you to forget about it." She hip-switched out of the room as quickly as an agile old woman could manage. Frankie, with the aid of his walker, rose and followed her out at a far statelier pace.

When they were gone, Clarice said in some distress, "Oh no. Have I made her mad? I'd hate to upset her." They all looked at Lily. As Eunice's roommate, Lily was the final authority on this matter.

"She's not mad, Clarice. Eunice just loves a dramatic exit and she so rarely gets the chance to do one anymore." Lily shrugged. "But I am sure she really means it. She would hate to hurt an old friend even at her own loss."

5

"I guess I'm glad she knew it was happening," Clarice admitted. "I like to know my clients are aware of their finances."

"Oh, she'd know all right. It's sometimes easy to think of her as flighty. But Eunice always knows what's up."

"Maybe," said Bear. "But this time, what's up doesn't just affect her. Others may be getting taken, too."

"Well, that's a good point, Bear," Lily said. "I'll talk with her about it when she calms down a bit."

"Might have to give this some thought," Bear muttered mostly to himself, struggling up with the help of his custom-made quad cane.

"Maybe there's a way to stop it without Louella Bowles even knowing that Eunice started it." Lily flashed a broad grin at him before he turned to walk away.

As he kachunk, kachunked down the hall to his room, Bear hummed a few bars of *Here We Come A-Wassailing* before he realized what the hell he was doing. He always hummed an oldie but goodie when he was thinking about a crime but not a damn Christmas carol, for God's sake.

Then another thought flitted through his massive head. It involved the Mona Lisa grin that Lily had given him as he left the living room.

Lily. Did she have something to do with this mystery? Did she set up that tea party? Had he just been conned into action? He damn well wouldn't put it past his conniving little assistant to do something just like that.

CHAPTER TWO

Case Notes
December 8, 9 p.m.

While the mystery percolates in Bear's brain for a while, there are plenty of other goings on around Latin's Ranch. I mean, it's the holidays and all. I don't know when the wedding will happen, but I do know where the stag party is slated to be. It will start with whiskey and poker in the trailer owned by Sam Hart, Jessica's barn manager. God knows where it will go from there. Might be wise to hide the Silverado keys that evening.

The wedding is for Jessica Winslow, owner of Latin's Ranch, and Bennett Stassen, her long time love. We'd all thought the wedding would happen before Christmas, but now it looks like first of the year. I don't think it has to do with the temperature of either one's feet. I think they just haven't had time to settle on the date and the plan. After all, they're up to their eyeballs in adopting a baby.

That seems to be ass backwards, but Ben's daughter, Rachael, wanted no part of raising her baby. She never even got around to naming the little tyke. So Ben took over the job, and Jessica opted to take on both Grandpa and Grandbaby as her husband and son. With a little push from yours truly, Boy Baby was finally named Benny.

Since Jessica has enough on her plate at the moment, we've all offered to take over holiday preparation. The aides have decked every nook and cranny with holly and fir. Charlie is baking and decorating

Christmas cookies. He's actually pretty good at it, but he's long gone from the kitchen before Aurora's workday begins. She scared the shit out of him one day with a wire whip when she caught him using her oven. Eunice is turning out one craft project after another. At the moment she's knitting what she calls the Ugliest Christmas Sweater Ever, sized for a baby. If there's a contest for that sort of thing, she might just win it.

Me? I addressed envelopes for the Latin's Ranch Christmas card. It features Jessica, Ben and Benny, five residents, three aides, one cook, one barn manager, Gina Lola (our oldest resident in horse years), a cat, a dog and two canaries. The copy below the photo reads: From our house, barn, kennel and cage to yours, Happy Holidays! *We pooled our lists of family and friends to receive the cards. All except Bear who said anybody he knew worth the cost of a stamp already lived here.*

Now that the cards are all addressed, I might suggest a visit to My Fair Pair to see what we can see. Eunice can convince Frankie to have Vinny take us. She could probably convince Frankie to take out half the population of the Pacific Northwest if she had a mind to. Vinny Tononi. That's Frankie's bodyguard, chauffer, and goomba. He's also my daughter Sylvia's boyfriend. Ms. Proper and Mr. Mob. Guess that's all the proof anyone needs that opposites attract. At least she isn't packing heat yet herself. Or dressing like a mobster's gun moll. I've seen enough wise guy movies to know those gals have a pretty questionable look all their own.

- Lily Gilbert, Elfin Assistant to PI Bear Jacobs

"Can a person die of an overload of happiness?" Jessica asked Ben in the darkness of the wee hours. Baby Benny was momentarily asleep on his grandfather's naked chest.

Jessica, equally in the buff, snuggled next to them both. She was delirious. Ben and she had become foster parents to Benny. In the fullness of time, with Rachael's okay plus good character references, nothing would stand in their way. Benny would be adopted by the new Mr. and Mrs. Ben and Jessica Stassen. He would be her son.

Being this over-the-moon happy terrified her. It had been damn hard to give her heart to another man, after her first husband's truck had skidded on black ice then plunged over a cliff to his death. And now she'd opened her heart to Baby Benny who was possibly damaged by drugs while still in the womb. She was setting herself up for more years of grief if anything happened to either of these two. It was scary just how ephemeral happiness could be.

"Can a couple elope with a baby in tow?" she asked.

"Yes and yes," Ben answered sounding more than ready to drift off to sleep.

"I thought my first wedding was hard to plan. But this one is way out of hand what with all the help from those five old wedding planners downstairs."

Ben nuzzled the baby's feathery hair. "Might I say that the suggestion box was not my bright idea?"

"Maybe not. But I'm thinking the suggestion about sipping liquid chocolate out of my navel was your idea. At least I hope it was."

Residents and staff alike felt free to give them suggestions. So Jessica had cut a slit in the top of a shoebox, labeled it 'Wedding Ideas.' To date, suggestions included 'give us kazoos, and we'll learn the Wedding March.' And 'gallop up to the altar on Latin Lover and Latin Dancer.'

The dourest suggestion came from Bear. 'Go with a zombie theme. Most of us are close to the grave anyway.' Jessica would be as glad as everyone else when he got over his holiday attack of the blue meanies.

She listened intently in the dark. It had become her habit ever since opening Latin's Ranch. She'd been surprised how much insomnia seniors dealt with. Someone was moving in the kitchen now, maybe getting cocoa or a snack.

Ben said, "Those old souls love to cuddle and coo. Benny didn't have the healthy start other babies get, but he sure has that."

"Yep. You're not just getting a wife. You're getting an army of babysitters."

He snickered. "An army with canes and walkers instead of humvees."

"And a golf cart they call Sitting Bull."

✦ ✦ ✦

Lily and Eunice spoke again about the issue at My Fair Pair when neither of them could sleep. Their beds were at right angles to each other in the same room, leaving plenty of space in the middle of the floor for Lily to spin her wheelchair. Eunice was knitting by the light of her nightstand lamp in the early morning hours, a pair of magnifying glasses perched on her nose. Lily was indulging in a secret pleasure. She just loved a thrilling bodice ripper. She was well into a bit where the plucky gal was fighting off the caballero before the fate worse than death when Eunice muttered, "If the hunk on that cover wanted to rip my bodice, I'd jolly well let him."

Lily snorted. "You mean you wouldn't defend your virtue?"

"Dear God, no. Virtue is largely overrated."

"Hmmm. How about the virtue of letting a friend be ripped off?"

For a while Eunice's knitting needles clicked as quickly as teeth chattering in the cold. Finally she answered. "I have no heartburn over Louella Bowles knowing about theft in her store. I just don't want her to know I'm the whistleblower. Or to think I want my money back. I won't personally hurt her, Lily, any more than I'd ever hurt you." *Clickety clickety click.* "But it would be just as well to get it stopped in case other customers are being hurt by it. And maybe there's even such a good reason why someone needs the money that it can be forgiven." *Clickety click.* "And of course I always love to go there to see the merchandise. We could get Jessica some sexy undies."

Lily took that statement as a green light for an investigation to begin. "Okay then," she said, figuring she'd bring it up to Bear at first light. She listened intently for a moment in the dark. "Is that Benny?" She cocked her head and stared toward the floor above. "Kinda wish Jessica would dump him with us the way Rachael did."

"Yes. She's being entirely too selfish with the little guy."

✦ ✦ ✦

After breakfast, the residents gathered in the living room to read the newspapers. They could get news online, of course, but they'd never gotten out of the habit of getting their fingers dirty with real ink. Two subscriptions allowed them to clip lots of coupons, and for Charlie and Eunice to giggle over the comics together. They read *Dilbert* and *Pickles* aloud to the others, each taking a character role or two. The double subscription also let Bear and Lily each have a crossword puzzle. Now they no longer fought over who got to it first, but who took the least time to complete it.

"Oh, look," Lily said spotting an ad and holding it up for all to see. "My Fair Pair is having a sale on nightgowns. Maybe I'll go take a look. Care to join me, Eunice?"

"Why yes! What an excellent idea!"

"Bear? Would you like to join us?" Lily asked.

"What?" He looked up from the sports page, having clearly ignored the conversation so far.

"Would you like to go with us to My Fair Pair? Maybe you'd pick up some clues about the theft that I would miss on my own." Lily would bat her eyelashes but she had virtually none left to bat.

Bear lifted his lip in a snarl. "What the hell would I need to go in there for? I know how the theft is being done. It's happening the way it can in a small store without many employees on duty at any one time. Either the owner is fiddling with the receipts after hours, or an employee is taking in cash and pocketing it. Don't need to go see a bunch of fancy pants to know that."

"I don't get it. Explain," Charlie said. Lily was not surprised that Charlie might be interested in a plot involving lady's undergarments. He was something of a womanizer based on the past relationship with his wife. A failed womanizer, as far as Lily was concerned. While she liked Charlie well enough, her own chemistry regarding the tall, high-voiced, loosejowled septuagenarian was anything but heated.

Bear looked up from his paper again and addressed Charlie. "Let's say an employee has Eunice's charge account number."

"No. Not my number," she said. "Someone else's number."

"This is just by way of example, Eunice."

"I don't care. Make an example of someone else."

"Okay, okay. A customer comes in and pays cash for an item. The employee rings it up on the cash register. After the customer leaves with her purchase and her cash receipt, the employee voids the sale then rings it in as a charge using Betty Jo Jean Applebottom's number. The cash register balances, the inventory matches the receipt, and no one is the wiser unless Betty Jo Jean Applebottom happens to notice it at the end of the month when paying her bills. Of course if the charge isn't too high, it may well slip under BJJA's notice."

Charlie sat for a moment, scrunching his features. Then he relaxed. "Got it. Clever."

"There are other ways. For instance, whoever closes out the cash register at night could be charging BJJA and just taking cash from the day's receipts. But that's easier to detect."

"So how would we know the guilty party?" Charlie asked as Furball jumped down to find a spot closer to the gas fireplace.

"Easiest way? Get the receipts, find the times that BJJA is charged, and see what employee was on duty then. A pattern would emerge. Or, without the receipts, somebody could probably check her own records to run down the time of false charges. If *somebody*," and here Bear cocked his head toward Eunice, "would allow me to work with Clarice, I'm pretty sure we could figure it out quick enough."

"Would that 'somebody' have to give her identification to the store owner?" Eunice asked.

"Nope. Not if Clarice just claims to have found the culprit herself."

"Would that somebody be able to know *why* her money was being taken?"

Bear took hold of his bottom lip for a moment then said, "Maybe. Maybe she could. With the help of her friends."

"Then maybe while we're in the store shopping, we could get a peek at an employee schedule," Lily said.

"That would be an excellent start. If somebody were to allow it."

"Are we still talking about Betty Jo Jean Applebottom?" Charlie asked, worry lines inscribed across his forehead. "I'm lost again."

The rest of them went back to their newspapers. Lily, not unkindly, whispered to Charlie, "No, Charlie. There's nobody named BJJA. Bear was talking about Eunice."

"I thought so. Well then. If the game is afoot, maybe I'll have to go with you to My Fair Pair. Don't want you two unprotected."

"No, Charlie," she said again, this time a little less kindly. "I think this is one crime scene that Eunice and I can handle alone."

✦ ✦ ✦

After Lily and Eunice left for My Fair Pair, Bear kept an eye on Benny so Jessica could work on Latin's Ranch bills. The baby was in his bouncy seat on the game table, and Bear was giving the little chair the occasional jiggle. He was reciting *This Little Piggy* when his cell phone started to ring. Bear frisked his body at every possible phone location until he found it in his left pants pocket. By the time he extracted it, unlocked it and growled, "Hello?" he'd missed the call.

"This little piggy went to damn it all anyway." Now he'd have to figure out voicemail again. "Wee, wee, wee," he said as he punched in a variety of combinations until he hit on the proper one.

The message was from Lily's daughter, Sylvia Henderson. "Hi, Bear. Could you give me a call? I have a favor to ask. Maybe you can help me with a problem."

Now what the hell is that about?

"Wee, wee, wee," he said again to Benny as he placed the return call. The baby's toothless grin resulted in a fine burp. "That's my boy," Bear said in admiration for the kid's accomplishment, just as Sylvia answered his call.

✦ ✦ ✦

My Fair Pair had opened its doors years ago with utilitarian women's socks, hosiery and under things, but as it had prospered so had its product line. Now it carried nightwear to panties in a wide range of naughty to nice. The attraction to pretty things, to feeling fine fabrics against the skin, was not limited by age. Eunice and Lily enjoyed the shop as much as women half their years, although Lily figured they probably giggled more.

"What the hell is that?" she asked staring at a snippet of velvet trim and webbing on a display table.

Eunice held it up one way and then another. "I think it's a corset, only key bits of it are missing. Maybe it's on clearance."

They moved on to the next table. The mannequin torso on it was twisted in a position that defied human posture. "Wouldn't that cord go right up your ass?" Lily reached out and snapped it.

"It would if your ass wasn't made of hard plastic."

"Besides, I thought thongs were sandals."

"Not anymore. We've come a long way, baby."

"Why Eunice! How lovely to see you." A woman who would fit none of these little pretties gave the octogenarian a hug against her DD breasts.

"Oh, Louella! You have so many beautiful things." Eunice fought herself free from the fleshy embrace and introduced Louella Bowles to Lily and explained why she rarely made it into the shop anymore. She told the storekeeper all about moving to Latin's Ranch and ended with, "Usually, I just call in an order. But today, we're on a mission."

Lily frowned. Was Eunice just going to flat out *ask* Louella if she was messing with her charge account? What kind of detective work was that?

"Lily needs to find a wedding shower present for our caregiver. I'm sure she'll find it here."

Lily breathed a sigh of relief. Eunice was playing the game just right.

Louella turned to Lily with a high voltage smile. "Well then! Let me show you our bridal collec – "

"- oh no, dear. Let's let Lily explore on her own while you and I have a chat. Does that work for you, Lily?"

"What a good idea! I'll enjoy a snoop, uh, look around while you two take your time." Lily peered to the left and to the right, seeing only two teenagers going through patterned socks. "Doesn't seem too busy at the moment. Are you here alone?"

"Weekdays before lunch are slow. Afternoons I need help." Louella took a look around. "Let me know if you need anything, girls," she chimed, but they mostly ignored her. She turned to Eunice. "Come on back here behind the counter with me. I'd love to catch up. I can unpack this order while we talk. She indicated an open box on the counter.

Louella set up a folding chair behind the sales counter for Eunice. The two began their conversation while the store owner lifted sports bras in a rainbow of colors out of the box. Lily was well aware Louella also maintained a raptor-like vigil on the two teens. She was also well aware that Eunice was speaking loud enough for her to hear what was said.

After a seasonal chat about old acquaintances not forgotten but rarely brought to mind, Eunice cut to the chase. "Lots of things to do as a shop owner, huh? Order merchandise ... check it in ... maintain records ... manage the books. Busy, busy, busy."

"Oh my yes. Especially at holiday time." The two teens left the store. "Add to that list keeping an eye out for shoplifting."

"Must take a lot of employees to keep things going."

Louella greeted an incoming customer, then said to Eunice, "Actually, just five of us work full time since we're closed on Sundays. My daughter Sami, you know her of course, and three others. Some extra help for the holidays. But customers like to take their time in here, shop without anyone hovering. Speaking of which, you doing okay, Lily?"

"Just fine!" Lily had moved from a display of French cuts near the counter to what she thought were the most beautiful slips she'd ever seen. She felt a flood of desire for one even though she couldn't remember the last time she'd worn a dress. Oh but wait! Sicilian night!

"Hard to keep track of employee comings and goings. I suppose you have to post a schedule to keep it all straight." Eunice said.

"Well, I do, in the back room. But it's the same most of the time. Doesn't change much week to week. And either Sami or I come in at the end of the day to close. Are you thinking of opening a shop?" Louella asked with a giggle. "Such curiosity."

Eunice brayed, her orange spikes bouncing. "Oh no, my dear. Just nosy. You know me! My working days are done. Now tell me, how is that lovely daughter of yours?"

Lily moved from slips to kimonos. The hanging garments gave her a little cover as she edged her way toward the backroom. There was no way she could get there without Louella taking notice. She needed an excuse. "Louella, I'm sorry to bother you, but do you a restroom I could use?"

"It's not for the public, but if you don't mind working your way around boxes of merchandise, it's back there ..."

Ta-dah!

"I'm pretty nimble for an old lady on a walker," Lily said. "No worries." She headed into the passageway to the backroom. It was part storeroom, part office, and a total jumble of incoming merchandise for Christmas. Boxes of silky, satiny, lacy items. Also, to Lily's surprise, some heavy looking winter scarves, leggings and mittens. Coats, too, for men as well as women. The store apparently carried snuggly items for the chilly months to come although she hadn't seen any on display yet.

Everything was heaped just in front of the restroom door around a tiny desk. And sure enough, a schedule was posted above it on a bulletin board. Lily sat at the desk chair, took a sheet of paper from her purse and copied down the employee hours. She allowed enough time to pass, then went back to the front, gathered up a garment and went to the checkout counter.

Next to the pile of sports bras, she spread out a beautiful lace and silk kimono, short in length but with wide luxurious sleeves. "For Jessica," she said to Eunice.

"Oh Lily! It's beautiful!"

Lily was pretty sure that, observant as Eunice was, she didn't see the lace-sided ruby satin slip that Lily surreptitiously added to her purchase. Louella gave her a knowing smile as she rang up the order.

CHAPTER THREE

Case Notes
December 9, 2 p.m.

I gave Bear my notes on the employee work schedule at My Fair Pair, and Eunice handed over her charge account invoices for the past several months. He had her highlight the charges that were not actually hers. When last seen, Bear was on his way to the game table in the living room where he could spread things out. He said since he had work to do, as well as a private call to make, I should make myself useful elsewhere and let him be.

He actually looked happy for the first time in days. I was so glad to see that twinkle in his beady eyes again that I didn't even tell him what he could do with his 'let him be.' Maybe the holiday spirit is filling me, too.

Before taking a cat nap, I spent a while doing the exercises Ernie gave me. I'm building up my strength and flexibility. Sure it's hard, but I have good reason: I'm going to walk again!

I met Ernie months ago when I entered a nursing home following my amputation. I was one sad puppy back in those days. BTW, the nursing home is where he and Clarice met, too, and they've been an item ever since.

Ernie was the physical therapist there, and he helped me build enough strength to shift from wheelchair to bed, to get into a car, to use a walker when it's more convenient than the chair. He's no longer at the nursing home but works for a therapy clinic, and he's preparing me for a prosthetic leg. Ernie says it would have been easier for me if I got the artificial leg right after the amputation, but at that time, I was far too sick and far too weak. It takes more effort to conquer the process all these months later.

One of the crappier lessons? Learning to put on the shrinker. "Don't tell Clarice you have a shrinker or she'll think it's a weight loss device," I said the first time Ernie suggested one. Then he explained it's an elastic sock that shapes my stump so it will fit the new carbon fiber leg when it arrives.

"This is a helluva struggle. Worse than a condom," I said trying to pull the damn thing on.

"I imagine so if you were under the impression that you put a condom on your leg," Ernie answered all deadpan and refusing to help.

Sometimes, he has me experiment with a temporary orthotic just to get the hang of the thing, how to put it on and take it off. How to simply stand on it.

"Care to dance? I could be the maypole," I said, holding out my arms.

"Long as there's no break dancing involved."

My favorite aide, Chrissie, stays right at his elbow when he's here, learning every trick Ernie knows for keeping my skin in shape. Old skin tears so easily.

It all takes time. And it aches. But I don't intend to give up. When I get my new leg, Ernie will be here to help me walk and to learn what he calls 'advanced gait training skills' by which he means using stairs, walking on hills, crossing uneven surfaces, stuff like that.

That's what he means by it. What I mean by 'advanced gait' is having freedom that I thought was lost for good. How wonderful is that? Watch out, Bear ... your eWatson is about to have access to crime scenes and hidey holes almost anywhere.

But for today, a lady's underwear store is as dangerous as it needs to get.

- Lily Gilbert, Walking Assistant to PI Bear Jacobs

"Let's see if I have this straight. You want me to find out what a mobster wants for Christmas?" Bear asked, having listened to Sylvia's request when he called her back. He couldn't hide the smile in his voice, but he bit his cheeks so at least he wouldn't snicker.

"Well, you know. I mean, I thought since Vinny likes you that maybe – "

"You mean like gold-plated brass knuckles? A black silk shirt? A green and red Kevlar vest?" He couldn't hold back the snort.

Bear heard Sylvia take a deep breath before she began again. "We've recently started dating, you know, and I want to give him something he'd really like. But also appropriate. I thought you could snoop a bit and find out what he –"

"Diamond cluster pinky ring? *The Sopranos* boxed set? Tommy gun in a violin case?"

" – might really appreciate. And thank you, Bear, for making this so easy for me."

Finally, the big man relented. He liked Sylvia and knew it must have been difficult for this proper lady to make such a request. Besides, she was Lily's daughter. If he didn't help, Lily would have his sorry old hide as a bearskin rug.

He told Sylvia that he'd discover what he could. Then he sat back in the chair at the gaming table and laced his fingers over his belly. Now he could actually chuckle aloud. The idea of Vinny and Christmas together was more than he could resist. Santa hat with a shank inside? Like a mobster would wear that around the other goombas.

All in all, he'd enjoyed the morning on his own. This much privacy didn't happen often at Latin's Ranch unless you were such a bellyaching sorehead that nobody wanted to be in the same room with you. It was a behavioral technique he'd been known to employ. Like, for instance, now.

He frowned to himself. Why was this holiday season upsetting him so? It wasn't just the commercialism, the relentless carols, the false bonhomie that was getting him down. In fact, that stuff was no more than a fluffy frosting hiding the real problem underneath. Nor was it missing family and friends, or memories of crime scenes and battlefields from his past. Those recollections haunted him year round, as much in July as in December.

This was something else. His mood had more to do, Bear finally surmised, with it being so close to the end of this particular year. The trail to the past was a great deal longer than the trail still ahead. He knew he was living through the dusk of his life. Bear wasn't afraid of death, but he didn't exactly welcome it. Not anymore. Because he had things to do now. Just lately, he'd begun to feel useful again. Maybe more than ever before. He thought about his team of geriatric operatives – his feisty one-legged assistant with her computer, a spiky-haired diva, a man whose balls were always sore from sitting in a wheelchair, and a retired capo who was still as dangerous as he was charming. Together this little team, with Bear in the lead, had taken on a couple of serious crimes in the past few months.

Bear had discovered there was something to be said for being what was euphemistically termed "put out to pasture." He could slip - or maybe limp - under the notice of authorities and antagonists alike. Hell, being old didn't mean being dead. It meant his whole team could say and do things that a younger group – or he preferred the phrase 'less experienced' – would not survive. Their bodies may be letting them down, but their minds were primed and ready, at least for now. He knew that wouldn't last forever either.

No local cop on any force had the whole day every day to reveal a truth that wanted to stay hidden. They simply had too many cases. But Bear and his gang had time to focus on one. He thought about the razor clams he used to dig for out on the coast. They fought damn hard to stay buried. Some cases were just like that, had to be grabbed and sucked out of the muck.

So why was he so melancholy? He scratched the top of his grizzled head. It had taken years to reach this level of crime detection and prevention. He was not bound by the rules any more, even bent them when he was of a mind to. But how many good days did he actually have left? He shouldn't waste them on crossword spats with Lily or poker with Sam. In a world gone crazy with crime, he needed to fight back. Somewhere out there a darkness needed his light to expose it.

He sighed and looked back down at the papers on the table in front of him. At least this little exercise involving a charge account fiddle was something. It was better than no detecting at all. It would do until the next big thing came along.

He had gone through Eunice's invoices and compared the days that suspicious charges were made with the days on the work schedule. He could now eliminate one of the employees altogether because she didn't work any of the days that charges were made. Another worked two of the days, but not the others so she, too, was an unlikely candidate. That left an employee named Melissa Sullivan and the owner's daughter, Sami Bowles, who each had worked all of the bogus charge days. And the owner herself had worked many of them or closed the cash register in the evenings. Bear had hoped he could eliminate her for the sake of Eunice, but Louella was a suspect, too.

"Crap," he said aloud to no one.

His phone rang again. "Grand Central," he mumbled as he frisked himself once more for the little phone. When he saw the call was from Clarice, he was pleased.

"I have a suspect list," he announced.

"And hello to you, too, Bear," she replied.

"Yeah, yeah. Hello."

"I just called to see how things were going. If you needed my help," Clarice explained. "But you already have suspects?"

She sounded jolly to Bear. But he'd put up with it if he had to. "What do you know about Melissa Sullivan? Neither Lily nor Eunice recognize the name."

"Why do you assume I would? Do you think I'm in that store all the time trying on unmentionables?"

"Clarice I'm not questioning your shopping habits, or where you and Ernie like to go in your spare time. I thought since you work for My Fair Pair, you might know the staff."

"As it happens, I do know Melissa. Nice woman, middle-aged, has an air of composure. Might even say competence."

"How about Sami or Louella? A crook in that duet?"

"Louella has run the store forever. I don't see what she'd have to gain from this sort of theft. Not really. But Sami?" She stopped for a while and Bear could hear what sounded like her tapping a pencil on a coffee cup. "Well, she's not far out of her teens, Bear. She fought the idea of college. I know her mother worries about Sami being aimless. And about her choice in friends. And spending more than she's making."

"Sounds like such an obvious suspect that it's too damn easy." Bear wanted to sink his teeth into something meatier.

"I thought that when something was obvious it was for good reason."

"Maybe. But it's no damn fun to investigate."

Clarice sighed. "Okay. I hope things get seriously complicated for you. Then you can stay interested long enough to help Eunice keep her money."

After the call, Bear thought about that coffee cup Clarice had been tapping.

Coffee.

Where the hell were the aides when you needed them? Where was Lily? Where were the rest of them? The big man looked around as though they might have snuck into the room. He sighed and hoisted himself up.

Guess a guy has to get his own drinks in this joint.

✦   ✦   ✦

Lily was applying postage to the Christmas cards at the dining room table. A stamped stack to her left grew as the unstamped stack to her right shrank. It had sounded easy enough. But she'd soon found that the trace of neuropathy in her hands had made this chore, well, a real chore.

Eunice was across from her applying bits of sequined felt to an elf on Baby Benny's Christmas sweater. She'd donned her own gay apparel that morning, too, wearing a sweep of lovely red silk with tiny green buttons shaped like holly leaves. A crystal-beaded barrette clung precariously to a couple of her orange spikes; Lily knew it was a product of her most recent craft craze, beading.

Next to Eunice, Charlie was reading the instructions on a rheostat he intended to install in his room. The three of them were sharing a plate of the gingerbread men and Russian teacakes that Charlie made late the night before after Aurora had gone home. Lily had to admit that he was handy to have around. He often did projects around Latin's Ranch that might have been on a husband's 'Honey do' list.

She was wondering if he'd consulted Bear or Jessica about the light switch when Bear kachunked into the room. The big man went to the coffee urn, helped himself, then pulled out a chair and plopped down. He was humming *I've Got the World On a String.*

Lily smiled to herself. Having a mystery seemed to be lifting his spirits, just as she'd guessed it would. She knew better than to mention his lighter mood, but she gave him the opening to tell them what was going on. "Oh, hi, Bear. Did you get through the schedule and the invoices? What have you discovered?"

"I know the people who *can* be guilty and have eliminated those who *can't* be."

Eunice could always be counted on for enthusiasm. "Wow! That was fast. You're really good, Bear!"

"Who's still in the running as the Christmas Klepto?" Charlie asked.

"The Holiday Hijacker," Eunice added.

"Santa's Sneak Thief." Lily couldn't help herself.

"Stop it, all of you," Bear growled.

"Stop what?" Frankie asked as he entered the room and sat down on the other side of Eunice.

"Stop the Christmas caper crap," Bear answered with the hint of a smile.

Lily moved the conversation along. "You're right. This is serious. How do we get from the people it can be to the person it is?"

"We'll simply have to shadow them all." Bear leaned forward, grabbed the last gingerbread man and bit off its head. After he swallowed, he said, "Here is my plan. We start our shadow details on the My Fair Pair staff tomorrow night, beginning with the daughter Sami. Charlie and Lily, you'll come with me. Eunice, you can't go. You know the target and could be recognized if we're spotted."

"That's already understood, Bear. I won't be the one to point the finger." For emphasis, Eunice wagged her finger like a metronome. Her bangles clattered together in protest.

Then Frankie said, "I'll stay here to keep my little dove company. But Vinny will take you on this mission if you wish."

Lily thought how lucky it was to have the long arm of the mob so close at hand.

Apparently, Bear did, too. He doffed an imaginary hat. "Thanks, Frankie. Store closes at eight tonight. We leave here at 7:30."

"Do we synchronize watches?" Charlie asked. He looked eager to spring into action although Lily knew his action-springing days were long gone.

Bear answered. "I doubt it will be necessary to synchronize, Charlie. We'll all be in the same car."

"Oh, right."

Then Lily asked Bear, "Who are we tailing tonight?"

"Tonight, it's Sami Bowles, the owner's daughter."

"And we start with her since she's the most obvious subject, right?" Charlie asked.

Lily was glad Bear didn't lose his patience but said mildly, "Wrong. We start with her because she's the one who works today and closes up the store tonight."

"Of course! Um, I have one more question," Charlie said.

He's irrepressible.

"You guys never invited me along before. Why tonight?"

This one stumped Lily. Charlie was a good guy at heart and there was no need to hurt him. The truth was that Charlie rarely plussed any situation based on his brain power so they often didn't include him. But tonight, Bear must feel like he needed Charlie on hand. And to Lily's relief, his reply to the old man was gentle.

"Charlie, we have no idea where Sami will lead us. Maybe to her home and no more. Maybe to the Mall or a gym or a sports bar. Since we don't know where, we don't know who will make the best tracker. Maybe Lily, maybe you, maybe all of us. This isn't an exact science. But we can use your help tonight."

Charlie looked like a joyful bloodhound as his jowls settled into a broad smile. "Got it! Glad to be of service."

Bear turned to Lily. "You need to clear this with Jessica?"

She cocked her head and pursed her lips for a second. "You know, Bear, I think she's so involved with Baby Benny right now, she's not even likely to notice we're gone. If she does, Eunice can explain. Besides, there's nothing dangerous going on. Why wouldn't we go out for an evening? What could go wrong?"

✦ ✦ ✦

Sylvia Henderson had never seen an Italian opera in her life, much less one about a kid visited by the Three Wise Men. However, Vinny Tononi seemed to think an Italian Christmas opera was the entertainment best suited for the season and for a lady such as herself.

Lady, hell. I want to bed him, not wed him. Sylvia thought this as a half dozen costumed characters warbled away on stage. *If he doesn't touch me soon, I'll swoon.* She figured she was thinking in rhymes in order to block out all that clamoring.

She knew Vinny was courting her in the old world sense of the word. A proper sequence of proper events before a proper betrothal. She, on the other hand, didn't want betrothed. As her friend Tony so bluntly put it, she wanted 'to make whoopie, beat the sheets, hit a homer, mount up and ride.'

She blushed, so near to Vinny there in the next seat. She was much too inhibited to reach out and touch his hand ... not until he made a move on her. So how was she ever going to 'seal the deal' as Tony would say?

Why did relationships always have to be so hard? And why the hell couldn't she stop thinking about the mobster's long elegant fingers only inches from her soft ample breasts there in the darkness of the Seattle opera house?

CHAPTER FOUR

Case Notes
December 10, 11p.m.

First let me say we're all okay. Of course, it's not nice to be called rabble-rousing troublemakers. And even before that happened, the evening was off to a pretty odd start.

Bear, Charlie and I left Latin's Ranch with Vinny right on time. Our surveillance mission was to follow Sami Bowles to see if she might lead us someplace that Bear could associate with a need for money, a reason for her to steal. You know, like maybe to Mr. Buds marijuana store where Sami was feeding a massive habit. Or to a private garage where her boyfriend was restoring a '66 Corvette at enormous cost. Or to a titty bar where she danced off a debt. The possibilities were endless.

Bear figured one of us might be able to shadow her depending on the type of place she chose. I suppose if we ended up at a back alley cock fight where everyone was armed to the eyeballs, Bear might have sent in Vinny instead of us. I wonder if Vinny knew that.

Charlie and I were sitting in the back of the Caddy while Bear was up front in the passenger seat. Way, way up front. It felt like a mile away, but if I really squinted my ears, I could hear them over the sound of rain on the roof. I get my best information by eavesdropping. I know. I should be ashamed.

The conversation I overheard between Bear and Vinny was just

plain odd. Two big tough men who never had a jolly moment in their lives. Here's what they said:
Bear (*looking out the passenger window into the rain all nonchalant-like*)*: So Vinny. Be Christmas soon.*
Pause.
Vinny (*seeming to concentrate on a particularly tough bit of driving*)*: Es true,* Signore Bear.
Bear (*swinging his big head toward Vinny which allowed me to see his face at an angle*)*: Got your shopping done?*
Now, really. As long as I've known him, Bear Jacobs didn't care about Christmas or shopping. And even if he was in an expansive mood, he's on Medicaid. They don't go in for spending splurges. So his question was damn odd. I mean, who asks a hoodlum about gift giving?
Apparently, Vinny thought so, too. He merely shrugged his enormous shoulders. But Bear didn't let him off the hook.
Bear: *Imagine you got a few things on your wish list, too, huh? A particular video game? Maybe a Seahawks jersey? Seattle's Best Coffee? I know. A couple of days in the sun away from all of us. Ha-ha-ha.*
Vinny rounded a curve a wee bit fast. I slid across the back seat and slapped up against Charlie like we were on a Tilt-A-Whirl. Judging by his absurd little grin, he was pleased about it.
Charlie: *Why Lily ...*
Lily (*still straining to hear*)*: Button your lip, Charlie.*
Way up there in the front, the sunglasses Vinny kept on the dashboard slid from his side to Bear's. Bear caught them. From where I sat, I could see him hold them up and examine them before returning them to Vinny.
Bear: *Not much use on a night like this. Sunglasses.*
I breathed a little easier. At least Bear hadn't taken complete leave of his senses. He could still detect that it was a typical frigid, wet December in Washington. By eight o'clock it might as well have been midnight in the dark department.
Vinny (*sounding wistful to me*)*: Yes,* Signore Bear. *The sun is nice. I miss it many days in this corner of the country. But my* padrone? *If he stay here in the rain, Vinny stay in the rain. Capiche?*

Bear: *Yep. I* capiche, *okey dokey.*
Vinny: *Are we then done with Christmas chitchat for this time?*
Bear: *Yep. Done as a doornail.*
I'll have to shake the meaning of that little conversation out of Bear later. In the meantime I turned back to the subject at hand. We'd arrived at My Fair Pair, and I was on point. Getting evicted came much later.

- Luck-Be-a-Lady Assistant to PI Bear Jacobs

Bear had to admit it. Three oldsters attended to by a thug in a Caddy didn't make the most invisible surveillance team in all the world. But in his decades of detective work he'd learned you made do with what you had. You could just as easily be below suspicion as above it.

He had Vinny stop across the street from My Fair Pair. By eight o'clock there was plenty of open parking. They watched the store until Sami Bowles escorted a last customer out the front, lowered a metal gate over the door, and turned out the store lights.

"She's not likely to come out the front now," Bear said. "Gonna use a back door."

Vinny anticipated Bear's comment. He was already moving the car to a lot behind the little row of retail stores. Bear could hear the gravel crunch under the tires in a counter rhythm to the rain on the roof. Vinny shut down the engine and they waited.

As they watched, a person came out the back door of each shop. Bear presumed they were the closers for the Village Fudgery, the Book Nook, Mama's Flowers and the other businesses in the row.

They waited. The windows began to steam up.

"Should we all hold our breath?" Charlie whispered.

Vinny merely turned the key to Accessory and lowered the windows a small amount. Instant de-steaming.

Charlie was impressed. "Wow. You guys are good. I suppose there are lots of problems on surveillance. What to eat. Where to pee. Stuff like that."

The mention of food made Bear's stomach growl. "Why don't you go knock over that fudge shop while we wait, Charlie?"

"Well ... okay." Charlie reached for the door handle.

"Bear's just kidding," Lily said, pulling on Charlie's arm. "Stay in the car. Don't open the door. A light will come on."

At that moment, their mark emerged.

"That her?" asked Charlie.

"Five foot six, blond, early twenties. That's how Eunice described her. I'd say she's the one," Lily answered.

"The fact she's coming out of My Fair Pair after hours is another good hint." Bear added. "I see she's changed clothes."

Sami had on a far flashier outfit than when they'd spotted her through the front window. Her dress was shorter at the hem and at the breast. Bear wondered how the hell the damn thing stayed down and up. Must be something to do with some arcane lacy thing they sold in there.

Over the sparkly little number, Sami had also donned a see through plastic raincoat.

"She looks wonderful. Sort of well-upholstered where it counts, you might say," Charlie said dreamily. "Just like her mother."

"You know Louella Bowles?" Bear asked, turning around to stare. "Why didn't you speak up before?"

Charlie's jowly old face almost managed a leer. His eyebrows definitely waggled. One of the things Bear liked about him was that he was no pushover, regardless of appearances. "Not anybody's bee's wax who I've seen a time or two in my past, Bear. Besides, I didn't want Eunice to know that I know more about her friend than her friend would want her to know that I know about her."

Bear stared a moment longer, working that comment out. He exchanged a glance with Lily. Then he turned his attention back to the target. Everyone was silent as they waited for Sami to load her large tote into a small Mitsubishi sports car. She got in, fired it up and thundered out to the street. After a moment, the Caddy prowled after her.

Sami's first stop was the night depository at the bank. It was no surprise. Clarice had told Bear which one My Fair Pair used, and whatever scam was going on, it wasn't with the deposits. But her next stop was an unknown.

Vinny followed her with ease through the dark and stormy night to the

Six Waters Casino. Bear knew it to be a lively place, owned and operated by one of the local tribes. But no matter how nice-looking it was, livelihoods were still lost in there. Gambling could be a dangerous habit if out of control. Was that a problem for Sami?

She found a parking spot right away and scurried to the portico over the casino entrance. There she stood shaking rain off her coat and fussing with her hair. Vinny maneuvered his starship up to the front entrance to offload his three old passengers along with their mobility equipment. Meanwhile, one of the valets greeted Sami by name.

"They know her here," Bear observed to Lily.

Unfortunately, in the transfer process, Charlie came down a little too hard on the seat of his wheelchair. "Eeeeoooouuuwww!" he shrieked. Bear knew he'd hear plenty about Charlie's sore nuts when they got back to the Ranch that night.

Everyone within twenty feet of the entrance turned to stare at them as the old man yowled. Valet parkers, security guards, and customers, including Sami Bowles.

"Oh dear, are you okay?" she asked, dropping her comb into her tote and trotting over to Charlie, weaving her way between the rest of the Latin's Ranch gang. She put an arm around his narrow old shoulders as he whimpered. "You poor man. What can I do to help?" Her breast nestled against his ear. He looked up and winked at Bear.

Bear nearly groaned. The target had actually engaged with the surveillance team. This was not first rate detective work.

"You come right on in with me, Mister." Sami continued, pushing the wheelchair toward the door. "Let's get you a drink." She glanced at Lily and Bear who were watching wide eyed. "Come along you two. You could use drinks, too."

Next, her eyes looked up, up, up until they reached Vinny's. His mass and demeanor apparently didn't intimidate her. "If you're supposed to be taking care of these people, don't you think you should be doing a better job of it?" Sami sashayed on past the muscled mobster.

"He might just off her!" Lily gasped.

Bear said, "Easy there, Vinny. She knows not what she says. Go park, then come in."

Vinny looked daggers after the offending girl and agreed only in part to Bear's suggestion. "Yes, *Signore* Bear. But I wait for you in the car."

"You're not coming in?"

"Es not a good idea, a man like me in a casino his *famiglia* does not own. I would be, ah, unwelcome."

Bear got it. Vinny was part of a dangerous underworld. He was entrenched in everything unseemly about the mob. He was a willing protector of the Latin's Ranch gang, but Bear never forgot this Dr. Jeckyll was a Mr. Hyde to the rest of the world. He would likely be on the casino's "no entry" list.

Sami pranced on ahead through automatic doors with Charlie in his chair. Lily followed and Bear brought up the rear. He battled with the wall of odors that attacked them. The smoke, the perfume, the over excited bodies in search of easy money. Bear sneezed but kachunked gamely forward on his quad cane.

As Sami weaved through the crowd, she yelled, "Out of the way, coming through," until she wound her way into the bar. "This man needs a drink, Bobby!" she commanded, coming to a halt in front of the bartender. "He hurt himself in the casino portico, poor baby. His friends may be hurt, too!" Sami nodded toward Lily and Bear as they entered the bar.

"Good heavens, Sami!" gasped the bartender, no doubt while visions of law suits danced in his head. "It's on the house for you as usual. And for all your new friends."

"There now, Mister. What's your name?" Sami purred as she wheeled his chair to a table and plopped down beside it.

"Char ... ah ..." Charlie came to a halt looking around wildly for Bear. The big man wondered if he thought he needed an alias. Why the hell?

"Char?" asked Sami, her eyes wide with question. "Oh, I get it! Char as in Prince Charming, I bet! What a giggle."

Charlie plumped up like a partridge. "Prince Charming. That's me!"

Bear sighed. At least Charlie's detective skills, poor as they were, had resulted in information they could use: Sami was well known in the Six Waters Casino. Well enough known that her booze was on the house. And the bartender knew her by name.

"Thank you, Miss." Charlie said weakly. "You are an angel."

"Call me Sami."

Bear and Lily introduced themselves as Bear and Lily. Then Lily went into Sweet Old Lady mode. "We're so pleased you took pity on Prince Charming, here. Life can be painful for the handicapped." Lily patted Charlie's hand.

"I can only imagine. But you all look quite capable to me." She made an expansive gesture out toward the casino floor.

Bear followed her gesture. He saw busloads of seniors muscling their way between younger guests, from poker tables to buffets. Over the whoops and beeps and bings of electronic noise and through the smoke haze, old voices occasionally rose above the fray, shouting things about baby needing new shoes or the heritage of any person who had stolen his or her slot machine. It had been a long time since Bear felt like one of the younger people in a room.

What is it that you play, here, my dear?" Lily asked, bringing Bear's attention back to Sami.

"Well, the slots, of course. Everyone plays them. But mostly I'm learning blackjack. I just love it."

"Really? How adventurous!" Lily cooed.

"Are you good at it?" Bear asked.

"No, not really," Sami suffered momentary sadness, like a teacup poodle told she was a bad girl. "They try to teach me and I try to learn. But I just can't seem to do the math for blackjack. I mean do I stop at sixteen or go to eighteen or what? You know? I can't add seven and six or nine and eight fast enough when I get nervous. But I'll get it one day."

Bear had heard all he needed to hear. The girl was a liability in a casino, no doubt about it. He now realized why she was the last closer to leave the row of retail stores earlier that evening. She probably had a devil of a time getting the register to balance.

Another round of drinks appeared out of nowhere. Sami stood to go. "You look okay now so I'll be on my way. Like they say, you can't win if you're not in. Lovely to meet you all." She waggled her fingers at Bear and Lily, then stooped to deliver a kiss to Charlie's cheek. "See you later, Prince Charming. Hope you're doing better."

"I am now," Charlie sighed, rubbing his cheek. The Latin's Ranch

Three watched Sami until she disappeared into the crowd.

"Sad," Lily said.

"Maybe she needs a mentor." Prince Charming said with a hint of a slur, then threw back his margarita to a cry of "Ole!"

Bear said, "Medications and margaritas don't mix, you old fart. You're getting hammered."

"Ain't it grand? First time in years."

"Besides, Charlie, if Sami needs a mentor, I'm the one to teach her," Lily said.

Bear stared at her. "You play blackjack?"

"I play it all. I was a dealer years ago in Vegas."

"You never said."

"You never asked."

Bear realized he'd learned something new about each of his operatives this night. Charlie couldn't hold his liquor and Lily could book the action on a casino floor. He reflected on inviting Lily to his poker nights with Sam Hart, the barn manager at Latin's Ranch. But no. She might win.

At that moment, Bear saw Vinny at the entrance, surrounded by security guards. "We're leaving. Now." He started to rise.

Lily struggled up immediately, grabbed her walker and headed for the door. When the chips were down, she was the best of soldiers and would not argue. But Charlie reached out and patted a waitress's nearly naked butt. She swung around, ready to slap him into another county. Only his sad face and wheelchair afforded him mercy. Charlie raised a hand and said, "I'm going, Mish." He tried to control the boozy slur but failed. "You's given dis ol' man great pleasure."

By then, Bear had left him and joined up with Lily. They rushed through the crowd, the racket and the lightshow. Bear was breathing heavily by the time he braced himself in front of the security team who circled Vinny.

"See here. What are you assholes doing?" he roared as loudly as a winded bear could roar. Bear was a formidable presence in the narrow walkway formed by the crowd.

"They take me from the car, *Signore* Bear," Vinny explained. "I do nothing wrong."

One of the guards put a hand on Bear's shoulder. "None of your business, *sir*. Now move away."

Bear wasn't leaving Vinny in the hands of security guards who might strip him of weaponry and dignity both. "Help!" he yelled to the crowd of onlookers. "Help me! I'm an old man! This guy is hurting me!" Bear crumpled over his quad cane, threatening to fall.

"Elder abuse!" Lily shrieked. The crowd was getting angry, filled with seniors as it was. It began to heckle. After that, Bear wasn't sure who was shouting what.

"Simmer down ... let go, asshole ... you crazy? ... get that walker off my foot ... hit me with a damn cane!"

Suddenly, the mob parted for a speeding wheelchair. "Hey! Youse guysh," yelled a pickled Prince Charming. "Waish for me."

"Jeez, another gimp," sniped a guard.

Charlie gave a mighty push to his chair and clipped the guard in the ankle with a heavy metal foot rest. The man went down like a ten pin.

Finally a manager appeared. She had her arms akimbo and was actually tapping her foot as though she were trying to emulate a grade school principal.

"He's mob, boss," one guard started to explain but Bear cut in, loud and clear. "They were holding our driver. We can't leave without him. Literally," Bear explained.

"That's right, miss," added Lily the Innocent. "None of us can drive."

"Awwww," said the crowd. "Poor old things."

The manager leaned in close to whisper to the three delinquents. "I don't care what is going on or what has happened, but here at the Six Waters Casino, we do not allow rabble-rousing troublemakers to conduct themselves this way. Do not plan on visiting us again."

"An' a happy holiday to you Mishes," Charlie slurred.

"What the hell is wrong with him?" Lily whispered as they headed for the door.

"He must have finished both of our drinks after we left," Bear replied.

Guards stayed with them until Vinny got the car, loaded them and drove away. Once off the casino property, Lily observed, "That went well."

"Actually, it did. We know that Sami is a regular at a casino and a poor gambler. Too much of that and anyone is likely to get in financial straits. And might steal from her employer, even if it is her mother."

"She's a sweet girl, though," Lily said.

"A suspect, nonetheless. But let's see what we discover when we track Melissa Sullivan tomorrow."

"Excuse please. Vinny speak now?"

Bear turned in the front seat to glance at Lily. She shrugged. So he turned back to the driver. "Sure, Vinny. What's up?"

"*Signore* Bear. You have plan, you execute plan. You need info, you get info. You take care of each other, you get me out. I think this es very organized crew. If I was not made man in the Sapienza family, I would wish to be Latin's Ranch family."

Lily rolled her eyes. Bear stifled a laugh.

Organized, sure.

"Well, we'll just consider you an honorary member."

"Es a great tribute, *Signore* Bear."

Charlie's raucous snore interrupted. Bear sighed. "His nuts may be sore tonight. But his head will feel even worse in the morning."

CHAPTER FIVE

Case Notes
December 11, 2 p.m.

Maybe all detective agencies have difficulty with their car pools, I don't know. But Bear had a surveillance vehicle shortage today.
Vinny was working for Frankie, probably something involving sleeping with fishes or going to mattresses. Whatever, he and his Caddy weren't available. The same was true for Sam Hart and Chrissie Metzger, both Latin's Ranch employees whom we've impressed into service in adventures past. They were working in their respective locations of the barn and the house.
Sitting Bull, our golf cart, would hardly do as an indiscreet way to follow a mark even on a gloomy day. Besides, it was far too cold for old bones like ours to go any great distance.
We had a personnel issue with operatives, too. Charlie was so tired from his adventure last night he was still in bed. Maybe alcohol was visiting him like a ghost of his Christmases past.
At last Bear said, "You know what you have to do, Lily."
To hell with that crap. "No, Bear," I said. "You know what you have to do."

- Lily Gilbert, Ornery Assistant to PI Bear Jacobs

When the phone rang, Sylvia was at her desk flipping through a heavy ring of damask fabric samples for the drapes in a conservative lawyer's office. The tones were subdued. Her interior decorator self shrieked *dull*. She considered it definite proof that the customer was not always right.

She answered the phone promptly, but before she could speak, the caller said, "Sylvia?"

"Bear?"

"It's me."

"It's me, too."

"Mickey Mouse."

Sylvia paused, plopping the samples down on her desk. She knit her brow. "Are you speaking in code?"

"Why would I do that?" Bear sounded confused.

"I don't know, Bear. When you said Mickey Mouse was I supposed to answer Donald Duck?"

"Can't imagine why. You asked me what Vinny would like for Christmas. I answered. He'd like something Disney like a Mickey Mouse. But subtle."

Unable to think of an immediate answer, Sylvia said nothing.

Bear continued. "Oh, and he misses sun on these gray days."

It was her turn again so this time she joined the volley. "Ah, how did you come up with that? I thought maybe something more, oh, romantic."

Even through the phone, he sounded peeved. "Sylvia, guys like Vinny don't get all starry-eyed when they talk to guys like me. But Mickey Mouse is sort of sweet, isn't he? Adorable? Isn't that close enough?"

"Oh, I'm not being critical, Bear. Well, not exactly. But why? How did you find out about Mickey Mouse?"

"Vinny's sunglasses. Expensive. Very macho. But they have a tiny gold circle with two tinier gold circles on the end-piece of the frame. The Disney logo. You know, mouse ears."

"But, but, doesn't everyone have some kind of logo wear? Seahawks? Hilfiger? Coach?"

"Not a mobster with a thing for cartoon mice. This is no coincidence. That tiny logo is a real brazen statement for a tough guy. Vinny could never admit such a thing to his boss. The other thugs would laugh and call him names."

Sylvia bristled. "Vinny is not a thug."

"Okay, sure. But for him to wear that logo at all, even miniscule on sunglass frames? I'm telling you, he'd appreciate something Disney that he could enjoy around you if not around Frankie. That's what he'd like. Trust me on this."

Sylvia sat for some time after she hung up the phone.

Disney?

That's what she got for involving a PI. Something totally unexpected. But she had asked for it.

She pushed aside the fabric samples and went to Google.

✦ ✦ ✦

Benny burped, strapped in his carrier in the back seat. Seated next to him, Bear did the same.

"Are you teaching each other nasty noises?" Jessica asked, raising an eyebrow in her rear view mirror at the happy twosome behind her. Benny was the only resident at Latin's Ranch who could always bring the big man around.

"Just sharing important guy stuff," Bear answered.

Jessica smiled to herself, secretly tickled. Bear had asked her for her help with one of his adventures. Always before it had been Lily. She was pleased that Bear felt comfortable enough with her to make a request.

As their caregiver, Jessica knew she must maintain safe standards. But she hated always being the stick in the mud. Most days, she kept her distance from his detective work. But today, she'd readily agreed to go along. Who wouldn't enjoy a follow-that-car exploit? Or a trip to a lingerie store? Besides, Jessica was up to here with wedding decisions and year-end Medicaid forms and child service interviews. A field trip with old friends was just the ticket.

"I must say, you were easier on Bear than you ever are on me," Lily grumped in the front passenger seat of Jessica's old Camry.

"Yes. Maybe because *his* request doesn't involve creeping around in the middle of the night or lying to the police or military-grade weaponry. Just one car following another. I'm happy to help."

"That's just what I told her, Jessica," Bear repeated in a tone far sweeter than usual. "That you'd be happy to help."

Lily shot him a finger gesture that would be more at home in a locker room.

Jessica pulled into the lot behind My Fair Pair on Bear's order. It was 2:30 in the afternoon. The three reviewed their next moves.

"Okay, Jess, we're waiting for a store employee named Melissa Sullivan," Bear told her a second time. "Her shift ends in about a half hour. But we don't know what she looks like for sure. Middle-aged and competent is all that Clarice had to say."

"I go into the store and take a look at the clerks so I can be sure the person who comes out is the right person to follow," Jessica said. "Check."

"Right, dear," Lily answered. "Another clerk is also working now, plus Louella. She knows me. So I can't go. I have to just sit here listening to the two burpers in the back."

"Walk around a store full of lingerie," Jessica said with a smile that deepened her dimples. Getting out of the Camry, she added, "This detective stuff is pretty darn easy."

She walked around the short block so she could enter the store from the front. It was busy with other Christmas shoppers checking their lists. Jessica suddenly felt a shiver of nerves, her confidence shriveling. It was as though a spotlight had caught her while a loudspeaker blared PERSON UP TO NO GOOD. She slouched in guilt, and she could feel her eyes get all furtive and slitty.

Crap. They'll think I'm here to shoplift.

Jessica took a breath, squared her shoulders and headed toward the counter. But a bridal display to the left caught her eye. And then her heart. Her nerves disappeared. She hit the brakes.

Ohhhh.

There was the most beautiful camisole!

Ahhhh.

She merely touched it and it drifted from the display into her hands. But then she saw the price.

Eouw!

This bridal stuff was as much as a *horse* bridle! Or a month of high energy grain. Or ...

"May I help you?"

Jessica whirled around and looked at the saleswoman. She struggled to tamp down her irritation over the price and to remember why she was there. The woman was middle-aged, well dressed, smiling. She didn't have the pillowy chest that Jessica had been told Louella wielded. The only other clerk in the store appeared to be too young. Besides all these clues, Jessica saw that the woman's name tag said, "Hi! I'm Melissa."

Melissa eyed the other clerks, too, following Jessica's glance. "Were you looking for someone else to assist you?"

"Oh, no. No. You'll do. I mean you're fine. By me."

Stop it.

Jessica started again. "Actually, I'm just looking."

"Would you like to try on that camisole you are holding?"

"Oh," said Jess, handing it to Melissa as though it were suddenly sizzling hot. Literally. "No, no. But your things here are lovely. I must come back when I have a bit more time to shop. For gifts." She raised an arm and looked pointedly at her watch. "Oh, goodness! Look at the time. Now, I must run."

Jessica left the shop in a quick step that would have made her stallion Latin Lover proud. She continued the pace until she rounded the block and got back to the car. "Okay, I'll recognize her when she leaves," she said to Bear and Lily, slightly winded. "And I'll never call detective work easy again."

✦   ✦   ✦

When Melissa came out the back of My Fair Pair, it wasn't quite what Bear expected. She was pushing a hand truck with two enormous cardboard boxes.

"If she's shoplifting she's being a little too obvious, don't you think?" Lily asked.

"And she's not alone," Bear added as the owner, Louella Bowles, followed with a hand truck of her own.

The three Camry spies watched while the two women rolled their bounty to an SUV. Melissa opened the back hatch, and together they maneuvered two of the boxes in. Then they slid another onto the back seat. When they finished, they gave each other a hug.

"Guess that's proof enough Melissa isn't stealing from Louella," Lily observed.

"That's some fancy deductive work," Bear sniped. He received the locker room hand gesture from Lily again.

Louella went back to the shop while Melissa fired up the SUV and left the lot.

"You're on, Jess," Bear said.

Jessica slid the Camry onto the street a car or two behind Melissa. The seasonal traffic was heavy and slow, so it was easy to follow. But as they drove out of the downtown and through the outskirts, the crowd began to thin.

"She'll see us following her now," Jessica said, concern making her voice a little strained.

"Don't worry, Jess," Bear said. "You can stay close. She has no idea she's being followed. Well, unless you rear end her."

This time, Bear received the finger gesture from Jessica.

"Don oo watch," he baby talked to Benny. "Mommy and grammy not nice to Uncle Bear."

Benny answered with a drooly smile.

They left the town's collar of fast foods and big box stores behind. The road narrowed to two lanes and began to serpentine its way upward through forested hills. By three-thirty, the dreary day began to give way to drearier dusk.

"I'll need to head home soon," Jessica said. "I'm the evening shift."

It was Lily's warning that brought the big man's attention away from the baby and back to the road. "Bear! They're turning. Look where."

The SUV bounced into the entrance to the county park.

As Jessica reached the same entrance, Bear warned, "Stay back now, Jessica. Give them room. Pull into one of these trailer spaces." On bleak winter days there were no campers in the park. The little Camry easily nestled into a camping spot with a circular drive.

"Think I know where they're going. Wait here." Bear hoisted himself out of the backseat and with the aid of his custom-made hickory quad cane, he ambled to a huge fir and peeked around its lowest boughs.

At the far end of the empty parking lot ahead of him, he saw the SUV. Melissa was opening the back. And coming to help her were several people. One was a man Bear knew only by the name of Ghost.

CHAPTER SIX

Case Notes
December 11, 8 p.m.

Well now, that was a surprise. Imagine Ghost rendezvousing with an employee from an underwear store. Ghost is a wild man, living rough in the woods after his years in the desert wars. We met him on a former case and learned that his moral compass isn't totally berserk even though it looks that way. He's a good guy, albeit a damaged one. It's a relief to know he's still out there, apparently doing okay. Jessica and I would have liked to say hello, but Bear said we'd better drive away and leave them to it.

"I've got a pretty good idea what's up," he said. "We'll finish this tomorrow." Benny agreed with a fretful snort.

I admit I was ready to go, too. I was tired. Sometimes these field trips get a bit long for me. And I still needed to do Ernie's exercise program. As Jessica drove us away, Bear call Sam Hart. "Can you drive us out to the county park ... no, in the morning ... with Sitting Bull ... yep, same place ... no, she's right here, and she says it will be fine ... really."

When he ended the call, Jessica said, "Pleased to hear how free you are with my staff's time, Bear."

"Sam mentioned what a reasonable boss lady you are."

I must say, I saw enough finger gestures in that car today to last a lifetime.

Bear told Sam to come up to the house when he was ready to go. Sam appeared after his morning chores with the horses, just as Bear and the rest of the residents were finishing breakfast. Aurora nabbed Sam, too, and sat him down with a plate of deliciousness. She often cooked Mexicilian recipes with the help of the resident Italian capo, Frankie. This morning she had upped her game another notch by serving an eggnog streusel coffeecake with slices of mild green chili frittata.

"The United Nations of breakfasts," Charlie claimed, pushing his wheelchair back from the table and patting the small mound of his belly. He smacked his lips then added, "How about a Mexican coffee to follow?"

"I do not think tequila and Kahlua are wise in the morning," Aurora answered with a stern frown and waggling finger. "Miss Jessica would say no so do not ask it again, *por favor*."

"Not too damn wise at night, either, Charlie," Bear said. "We'll stay away from casinos for a while if a little booze makes you crazy."

Lily chuckled. "Geezer gone wild."

"Hey, I think that waitress really liked me. Besides, you got what you needed," Charlie pouted. "You now know that Sami Bowles is a genuine suspect."

"That's right, Charlie. And if you hadn't played the drunken senior card, we might never have figured it out." Lily's eyes twinkled.

"Thank you, Lily, for recognizing my true acting ability." Charlie totally missed the sarcasm that Bear clearly heard.

The big man snorted a chuckle then addressed the group at large. "Yesterday we watched Melissa Sullivan remove large boxes from the shop. You'd have to suspect theft, but Louella Bowles was right there helping her. The two of them were up to something. We just didn't know what."

He paused for coffee and Lily took over. "We followed Melissa to the county park where our old friend Ghost met the delivery."

Frankie asked, "This Ghost. Es friend of Vinny?"

"Yep. That's the one," Lily answered.

"He is no thief, I think," Frankie said.

"I agree," Bear added. "I doubt he traffics in stolen goods or false charges. At least not knowingly. But I need to talk with Louella."

"I've told you I've known Louella a long time," Eunice's mascara-laden, eye-linered, blue-shadowed peepers looked ready to spring a leak. Bear panicked.

Jesus! She's gonna cry! Ahhh!

But she didn't. Eunice continued, composure intact after a blink or two. "Louella's husband is dead, her son went missing years ago, her daughter is not living up to her potential and may never. I do not want any part of hurting her. She's suffered enough."

"Of course not, Eunice. We know," said Lily. She patted her friend's bling-fingered hand.

Bear felt a clutching in the vicinity of his heart.

Indigestion?

No. It seemed to be genuine affection for the old girl. "That's a given, Eunice. We're not out to hurt her. Or you." In a fleeting moment of holiday cheer, the big man with the silvertip beard and the old woman with the orange spiked hair smiled at each other.

"Break it up, you guys," said Sam, before gulping the last bite of frittata, standing and throwing his napkin on the table. "Time to get underway so I can get back to work. It's pouring out there so wear your raingear."

✦ ✦ ✦

Bear, Lily and Sam had been at this very spot in the county park's parking lot before. They'd unloaded Sitting Bull from Sam's trailer back then, too. They followed the same path into the woods toward the same destination. The only difference this time was that Sam joined them, riding in the golf cart's back seat. And they weren't afraid of what might be watching them from the woods. Bear knew the destination.

When they emerged in the clearing, their raingear was soaked from all the boughs and vines that overhung the trail. But it wasn't actually raining so Bear removed his ancient rain hat, the one with the Seattle Rainiers logo. Sam and Lily pushed back the hoods of their slickers. A watery sun was doing its best to break through the Washington gray.

In front of them was a homeless camp of a dozen or so tents. Each stood on wooden planks or pallets to help keep them dry even though mud surrounded them. Two had tinsel Christmas stars mounted above their flaps. The tents formed a crescent around a large picnic table. Near it, a campfire crackled happily as a youngster fed it split logs. A large fragrant pot bubbled away on an old beater of a grill, filling the meadow with the aroma of soup.

Bear recognized the big boxes that Melissa and Louella had hauled from the store. They were open on the picnic table. Three women were removing mittens and scarves from them then distributing the woolens into several plastic tubs on a bench. Two of the women glanced up then returned to work. Only one came toward them as Lily, Bear and Sam dismounted from Sitting Bull.

"Lily. Bear," said Rita the Tent Master. "What brings you here?" She smiled although Bear could see the wary cast to her eyes. He had worked with this tall, rawboned woman to save two young sisters and to house an undercover cop. He admired her aura of authority. She kept her illegal camp in good working order, free of drugs and crime as much as was possible with its downtrodden population.

He reached out a paw for her hand and after a pause she took it. "Good to see you, Rita. This here cowboy is Sam. We're not here to cause you any trouble."

"You're not here for the exercise, either." Rain began to patter again.

"No, we're not." He cocked his head toward the table. "We need more information about the things in those boxes." The other two women cast frightened glances at each other, but continued working. Together, Lily and Bear told Rita how they'd come to follow the path that led back to her home. By the end of the tale, they'd settled on a bench, a new one that Bear knew had been made by his friend, Deputy Jo Keegan. Sam upended a firewood log and sat on it.

When Bear finished talking, Rita nodded, staring into the fire. The rain increased its patter. Bear wanted coffee. He was cold. His feet were wet. He needed a more comfortable chair. How awful it would be to live this way.

Rita's eyes were steely as ball bearings when she looked up at him. "I will trust you, Bear, if you promise you intend no harm to anyone involved."

"Promise."

She swung her head to Sam then Lily and stared a few more of those ball bearings.

"Yes, ma'am. Promise." Sam drew his cowboy hat lower over his eyes. Rain splashed off its brim.

Lily also promised, adding, "The woman who asked our help with this wants no more publicity or disruption than you do."

"All right, then." Rita began, her strong voice as captivating as a radio commentator. "There are many societies living in the deep forest. Like us, the homeless, of course. We come together here and try to help each other. But there are many others, too, some safe and others very dangerous."

"Dangerous?" Sam asked.

Rita nodded. "I know of a small group of convicted sex offenders who have gathered together. Communities move them out. They can't find work so they join up out here. Of course, we don't accept them either." She glanced at the boys splitting logs.

"Jesus," Sam muttered.

"There are groups of survivalists, too, that include women and children. And soldiers living rough and alone, no desire to belong. The woods can be a dangerous place. People die from exposure or from each other. Most public aid programs don't reach us out here. And most of us can't get to them. Or won't reveal our identities to take part. "

She pushed a soaked tendril of grey hair out of her face, anchoring it behind her ear. "A while back, a woman named Louella came to me. Several people here saw her, but nobody knows who she is. She offered help. It's not my business how she provides goods. Only that she does. Some questions are better not asked."

"Understood," Bear agreed.

"I still have the cell phone you gave me. She calls when there will be a load for us to pick up at the parking lot. She sends a person named Melissa with boxes of warm coats, mittens and socks, hats and scarves, sleeping bags. Everything new and clean, some of it for men but most for women. No insects, no tears, no mildew."

"And Ghost?"

Rita reacted with a grin. "So you know about his involvement, too, you old gumshoe. Yeah, he helps bring stuff here. But he doesn't know where it comes from either, just that it arrives. Occasionally, I can talk him into keeping some of the socks. And once a vest. He's over there in the woods watching us now."

As hard as he squinted, Bear could not see the wild man.

"We divide the stuff and fill these plastic tubs. Then Ghost takes them deep into the forest to the camps that need them. He gets close to places too dangerous for us and leaves the tubs where they'll be found. Nobody fears us, but everybody fears him."

Bear had learned all he could from Rita and taken enough of her time. He'd like her to know that he admired her. Maybe she already did. He wished better than a homeless life for her, but he knew that a bare bone existence was all that many people could handle. Not only soldiers battled PTSD. "Thank you, Rita," he said. He struggled up while Sam offered a hand to Lily. "We have all we need. We'll leave you to it."

"You won't stop the process?"

Bear shook his head. "That's not my goal. But I need to speak with Louella. You understand?"

"So you know who she is."

He nodded.

"I trust you to keep our wellbeing in mind." Rita made a gesture toward the others. "And don't tell her that you got her name from me." She rose and went back to work as the trio of interlopers crossed the soggy meadow toward Sitting Bull. Lily said, "This is the highest form of charity, I think. Supporting those clinging to humanity's lowest rungs."

Bear made a low growly noise as he mounted the driver's seat.

✦ ✦ ✦

That evening, Vinny drove Bear and Lily to My Fair Pair. There was no need to watch the back door, so he parked in front.

Lily was sulking. As Bear got out of the Caddy, she said, "Once again, I sit and wait. I want to go in, too. How can I do good case notes if I can't go in?"

"Not this time, I'm afraid. Louella will associate you with Eunice. We can't have that."

"I know, I know. Go ahead." As he shut the door, Lily crossed her arms and sunk deep into the cushy back seat. But that didn't mean she needed to sit quietly, wasting time with nothing to say or do. In fact, she had plenty to say.

"Vinny." She saw his shoulders square a bit more.

"Yes, Miss Lily?"

"You remember when you had that conversation with Bear about dating my daughter?"

His squared off shoulders squared off the least bit more. "Yes, Miss Lily."

"You know Bear is not the head of my household, don't you?"

"Yes, Miss Lily."

"Then I'm the one you should be talking to, Mister, when it comes to Sylvia."

Vinny sighed and sagged. Slowly, he turned in his seat to face her. "In the old country ..."

"Old, schmold. We're here. This is now. So what's the deal? And don't go all mobster need-to-know-basis on me."

"Your daughter ez real lady, Miss Lily. Sweet. Lovely. I would like to court her." He lifted one brow. "I *am* courting her."

"Yeah, Bear told me. But you know she's had sorrow in her life, yes? No real father? No steady home? A husband who was not totally faithful? One who died too young?"

"I am getting to know these things about her." Vinny's angular face tightened. "I would kill such a man who would hurt her, except that he is already dead."

"Fine then. You understand that I will kill you if you hurt her, too?"

"I would expect nothing less."

"Then I want you to know you have my blessings. Whether you marry or not. I want my daughter to have more enjoyment out of life. She's far too young to be at the end of laughter."

"So … you would accept Vinny?" Now a smile threatened his lips.

"Not important. What's important is that she does."

"Would you think I could, uh, demonstrate to her my affection in an open way?"

"Oh, for the love of god. Vinny, she's fort … um, not a kid. Neither are you. You know what you want. Don't make her guess. Time is too precious."

"Thank you, Miss Lily, for this confidence in a man such as me." Vinny actually beamed.

"It's quite all right, my dear." Lily wondered just how many mothers accepted an assassin into their families. Ah well. Tis the season of the lion and the lamb.

"And Vinny, one more thing."

"Yes, Miss Lily?"

"You might not tell Sylvia we had this little chat."

✦   ✦   ✦

Bear kachunked into My Fair Pair just before its closing time of eight. According to the schedule, Louella was handling the store alone that night.

"Hi! Just about to close," Louella chimed. "But I'm glad to help you." She walked toward him and tilted her head. "Christmas shopping?"

Bear thought she looked most agreeable. Maybe it was the facial expression that was too open to be insincere. Or the sprig of holly she'd woven into her auburn air. He'd always had a thing for redheads. "Ah, well …"

Louella's eyes smiled as she said, "Shy, huh? Lots of gentlemen are. You needn't be. We have many lovely things." She swept her hand toward a display of matching naughties.

Bear wanted to cover his eyes. "No. Not that. My named is Bear. PI Bear Jacobs. I'm here to talk about the accounts you're pilfering, Mrs. Bowles. And about your connection to the camp out in the woods."

Louella turned as pale and still as stone. Bear thought she resembled a frightened nymph caught in Michelangelo's marble.

But then the starch left her spine and color rushed back into her face.

Louella looked more like a startled doe. "I guess I knew it would happen one day. But I expected the police. Not, ah, you." She sighed then locked the front door and turned off the lights. "Come back to my office. Nobody else is here to interrupt us."

Bear had a wild thought about a ball bat behind the door. Or a gun hidden in the desk drawer. But it seemed so unlikely he followed Louella into the backroom. Besides, he could protect himself. There was always that dagger sheathed in his trusty quad cane.

She indicated the heavier desk chair for Bear. Then she removed a stack of lacy things from a folding chair and sat. "Where do I start?" Her hands began folding the frillies. One knee jiggled.

Bear hoped his own calm would help her settle. "Just begin, Mrs. Bowles. This isn't an inquisition. Take your time. I'll just ask questions as we go along."

"Fine." She placed the folded stack on her desk, stood and went to a Keurig machine. As she spoke she created two large mugs of decaf from two tiny k-cups. "I've had this store for many years, Mr. Jacobs. I'm nearing the end of my third decade as a matter of fact." She stopped and looked defiantly at Bear. "It might seem frivolous to some, of course. But it's always been important to me to make every woman feel pretty as well as comfortable."

"Admirable. And call me Bear."

"Bear. Right. Lately, I began to think about the needs that others have. Not for pretty, maybe, but for simple warmth. And not only women. Men and children, too. It occurred to me that I was in a unique position to give that away. Warmth." She handed him a china mug. He was worried he might break it. Fragile wasn't his strong suit.

Louella sat with her own mug and continued. "I could get my vendors to provide product lines I don't really carry here. Coats and heavy woolens. I could buy snuggies of all kinds at cost. Less than many charities have to pay." She looked excited as she talked but then saddened as she said, "My friend Melissa was willing to help. She works here, you know. But I couldn't afford it all on my own."

"And that's why you put the charges on customer accounts," Bear prompted.

She looked up from the mug cradled in her hands. "My, you do know a thing or two, don't you? Yes, I did. But I only took from those who I knew could afford it. And not much at a time. I hoped it would go unnoticed."

"It didn't."

"Apparently not. Who told you about it?"

"Not important. But, you just did it for altruism?" Bear asked before sipping the decaf. He trusted it wasn't poisoned. "For the spirit of giving? The betterment of mankind?"

"Well, no," she said. "Not just that."

"No?" Bear was rarely so far from the mark. "Then why?"

"To comfort my son. He lives out there in the woods. He gets cold, I know. But he won't take charity from me. He doesn't feel he deserves it." She shrugged. "This way he gets it without knowing it. Rita makes sure he's okay."

"You provide for a mass of people in order to provide for just one?"

"It's all I have of him. He's as much of a ghost to me as he is to anyone else."

Bear nearly gasped. "Ghost is your *son*?"

"You know him?" Now Louella looked surprised. No longer a statue ... no longer a startled doe ... now a loving mother. "Oh, Mr., ah, Bear. After the war my boy was so different. Damaged. Wouldn't come home to stay. But I know he still needs my help even if he doesn't know it."

Bear smiled. "He's a fine man, Mrs. Bowles. He's saved lives of people who matter to me. I would do a great deal for him, too."

Louella leaned forward and touched his arm. "Then maybe you can help me out of this mess. Everything got out of hand." Bear was sure her anguish was genuine. "I can't just stop now that so many depend on me. But I don't want to be a thief. What can I do?"

Bear's arm felt warm where she'd touched it. "I believe several of us are willing to help."

CHAPTER SEVEN

Case Notes
December 24, 8 p.m.

It's Christmas Eve. The tree in the living room is artificial because Jessica is afraid to have a real one in an adult care home. Fire danger, she says, and I tend to agree although she might be surprised how fast we could haul our old asses if need be.

Eunice and I gave her the silk and lace kimono from My Fair Pair earlier today since it's more a wedding present than a Christmas present. She cooed and sparkled and blushed like any bride-to-be should. She and Ben have decided on mid-winter for the actual event. They hope the adoption from the foster system will be settled soon after that.

Sylvia surprised me early this week. She brought over four boxes of my Christmas ornaments that she stored after my house was sold. It has been like a reunion with old friends to see them again, here in my new home. A home where, other than the plights of old age, I've been as happy as I've ever been.

She probably thinks I don't know it, but Sylvia surprised me a second time, too. She announced she would be gone the week after Christmas for some 'R and R at a fancy spa.' Then Vinny up and asks Frankie for the same week off to 'take his nephews to Disneyland.'

Uh-huh. I tracked down Bear. He finally explained his weird questioning of Vinny that day on the way to My Fair Pair. Appears that my daughter acted on his suggestion. I suppose the nephews may actually get to go. Sylvia might have figured it was the only way to get Vinny to agree. He'd demand a good cover story. Hope she had the sense to book the right number of rooms at the Magic Kingdom. There are wrapped gifts under the tree since we give each other little things, and we exchange with the staff as well. We have way too many packages for Baby Benny, too, but who's gonna tell the likes of us that we shouldn't dote? There's no chance in hell the kid won't grow up spoiled rotten.

The packages from Bear are easy to pick out because he always uses the Sunday comics. This year, crafty Eunice wrapped hers in old Christmas sheet music and made bows from puffs of red and white yarn dusted with green glitter. I'm hoping the little tins from Charlie hold the same honeyed pecans he made for us last year. Yum. I won't know until tomorrow morning, but you're never too old to speculate about what is hidden from sight.

I bought a handful of polished Australian agates for Eunice to use in her jewelry making and a downy soft throw that Charlie might find comfy to sit on. For Bear, I found the perfect folder to hold hard copies of all my notes on his cases. Judging by the shape of the gift wrapped in Doonesbury and Dilbert, he might have gotten the same thing for me.

Bear has seemed content lately ever since the My Fair Pair situation was resolved. Not exactly jolly, but not morose either. The darkness that dims his holidays seems to have passed. I knew a mystery to solve would help him. I'm surprised how much it's brightened things for the rest of us, too.

After his confrontation with Louella, Bear was convinced that the money she was siphoning was for a good purpose. But it was theft nonetheless. We talked with Eunice, then everyone else. Here's what was decided and enacted with universal approval:

Eunice will pay for the whole thing to keep it going on the right side of the law. "People need to be warm and dry. It's that simple," she said while putting the finishing touches on one of her yarn bows. "But I still don't want Louella to know that I'm involved. I won't embarrass her that way."

So Bear set up a Secret Angel process.

Louella promised to quit adding false charges to customer statements. In return, she'll receive cash from Eunice to cover all her "Project Forest" expenses. Clarice just puts it in the Miscellaneous column.

Bear, with the help of Sam or Vinny, intends to deliver the cash every month. Melissa will still take the goods to the county park. Rita 's group will still take it to the homeless camp. Ghost will still distribute. Louella still helps her son. And Eunice gets the genuine pleasure of helping an old friend, no questions asked. Win, win, etc.

Personally, I think this case is damn near a perfect Christmas story, what with people helping each other and all. Oldsters like me occasionally need proof that not everyone is an asshole. It gives me a kind of hope for humanity at large. We may yet be of goodwill, one warm pair of socks at a time.

- Lily Gilbert, Merry Assistant to PI Bear Jacobs

THE END

Author's Acknowledgments

For factual content in *Bear Claus*, I am indebted to many experts, librarians and websites. Any mistakes made are my own.

For critiques that range from sweet to pit bull in temperament, I am sincerely grateful to members of my critique group including Beth Pratt and Heidi Hansen. Without the valued support of Donna Whichello (my researcher, editor, and sister), the gang at Latin's Ranch would not exist. Thanks also to Vanessa Indelicato for her unflagging support with social media. Finally, I am indebted to Bear, Lily, Eunice, Charlie and the rest of the Latin's Ranch crew who continue to capture my imagination.

Finally, a doff of my verbal hat to my readers: you are the cheerleaders who keep me going. I hope you enjoy reading the PI Bear Jacobs series as much as I enjoy writing it.

About the Author

Linda B. Myers won her first creative contest in the sixth grade for her *Clean Up Fix Up Paint Up* poster. After a Chicago marketing career, she traded in her heels for rain boots and moved to the Pacific Northwest with her nervous dachshund and a grumpy parrot. You can visit with Linda on her blog at www.lindabmyers.com or on her author page at www.amazon.com/author/lindabmyers

The Bear Jacobs Mystery Series

Available on www.amazon.com

Meet retired PI Bear Jacobs, his eWatson Lily Gilbert, and the rest of the quirky residents at Latin's Ranch Adult Family Home in the Pacific Northwest. Yes, they are infirm. Yes, they gripe. But all the while, they solve crimes, dodge bullets and stand tall on their canes, walkers and wheels. Enjoy this whole series of cozies with bite.

Book One. **Bear in Mind**

The Latin's Ranch residents investigate the case of Charlie's missing wife. Is she a heart breaking bitch who abandoned her hubby? Or is a madman attacking older women? When others in the community disappear, Bear and his gang follow a dangerous and twisted trail to a surprising conclusion.

Book Two. **Hard to Bear**

A vicious crew is producing old-fashioned snuff films with a violent new twist: custom-order murder for sale. The Latin's Ranch gang takes on the villains behind this updated evil, coming under danger themselves. Bear joins forces with an avenging mob family, a special forces soldier tormented by PTSD, and a pack of mad dogs on the loose in the Pacific Northwest woods.

Novella One. **Bear Claus**

PI Bear Jacobs is mired down with seasonal depression until his e-Watson, Lily, finds him a mystery to solve. The trail is both fun and fearsome as it leads from theft in the My Fair Pair lingerie shop through a local casino to a dangerous solution in the Northwest Forest. Bear Claus is a Christmas novella.

Book Three. **Bear at Sea**

When Eunice wins the Arctic Angel Award, the Latin's Ranch gang cruises to Alaska to pick up her prize. But high life on shipboard is dashed by low life murderers and thieves. One of their aides is struck down, and Eunice's life is threatened not once but twice. The gang takes action, endangering themselves to solve the case of the short-tailed albatross.

Check Out Linda's Other Novels:

Fun House Chronicles

Self-reliant Lily Gilbert enters a nursing home ready to kick administrative butt until the chill realities of the place nearly flatten her. She calls it the Fun House for the scary sights and sounds that await her there. Soon other quirky residents and caregivers draw Lily and her daughter in as they grapple with their own challenges. Lily discovers each stage of life can be its own adventure with more than a few surprises along the way. The characters in the Bear Jacob Mystery series made their first appearance in *Fun House Chronicles*.

Lessons of Evil

Oregon, 1989. Psychologist Laura Covington joins a community mental health department. One of her new clients is so traumatized he suffers Multiple Personality Disorder. Through him, Laura discovers a desert cult and the vicious psychopath who commands it. Laura has unleashed dangerous secrets and now, she must decide how far she is willing to go to protect everything she loves. This is psychological suspense geared to keep you guessing as it builds toward its unpredictable conclusion.

A Time of Secrets: A Big Island Mystery

Life is uncomplicated in a Big Island village until Maile Palea, an 8-year-old girl, disappears. Twelve years later she is still missing. This is the story of her sister and brother who never give up trying to find her and cannot heal until they do, of a village that no longer feels safe from a changing world, and of a perpetrator who discovers what disastrous things happen when you keep secrets too long. A perfect read for fans of edgy suspense and hot Hawaiian nights.

The Slightly Altered History of Cascadia

First Female and Old Man Above have screwed up in the creation of humans and call on the spirit Cascadia to fix it. With the help of her human familiar, a magic blade, a flying bear and a logging horse named Blue, Cascadia takes on a killer, ends the traffic in bear gall bladders, and leads a war against a survivalist group intent on slavery. She devises a plan for a better kind of human. Will the gods agree or scrap the whole damn planet? This satirical adult fantasy is a fast-paced quest through history, mythology and modern day ills.

Visit with Linda B. Myers at

www.LindaBMyers.com
facebook.com/lindabmyers.author
myerslindab@gmail.com
amazon.com/author/lindabmyers

66448236R00037

Made in the USA
Lexington, KY
14 August 2017